Afsaneh • One from Many

... Invitation to Dialogue

AF208622

E pluribus unum • *One from Many*

• *For all,*
whose true stories
are part of this tale

Thanks to you, Afsaneh

Afsaneh

One from Many

یکی از همه

افسانه

2024

Vera Ansén

Bibliografische Information der Deutschen Bibliothek
Die Deutsche Bibliothek verzeichnet diese Publikation in der
Deutschen Nationalbibliographie; detaillierte bibliografische
Daten sind im Internet über http://dnb.dnb.de abrufbar.

The following story is a work of fiction. Any resemblance to living
or real persons may be in the eye of the beholder,
but is neither intended nor relevant.

Erstauflage: November 2024

Graphik und Gestaltung: Vera Ansén
Lektorat: Rebecca Ansén
Verlag: BoD · Books on Demand GmbH,
In de Tarpen 42, 22848 Norderstedt
Druck: Libri Plureos GmbH,
Friedensallee 273, 22763 Hamburg

ISBN: 978-3-7693-1572-1

Seek and Find within:

Her Invitation

My beloved sister,

it has been a long time since the same fire brightened our faces. I miss your eyes alight as we listened to the stories of the elders, and your laughter that so beautifully awakened my senses.

When I hear the birds in the early morning, chirping and singing with joy to greet the new day, their untamed zest for life fills me. I remember how we spread our arms and ran wildly around. Enchanted by the thought that if only we were light enough, we could fly like the birds, so endlessly free. The world was our home. We knew no boundaries, no obligations, no laws — only the love of our mother and her sometimes stern gaze that made us pause when we were too wild.

The moment we held our own children in our arms, whom we wanted to love and protect, that lightness of those days was gone.

As our mother, full of wonder, first looked into our eyes. Full of curiosity about what we might bring into her life. She knew we would not be like our siblings, that a different fate awaited us. That each child finds its own melody and its very own journey through life. All we can offer is loving encouragement toward good thoughts, good words, and good deeds.

None of us endured the hours of birth just to lose this life to any war, not to hatred among siblings, not to the battles of men, not to the interests of power. To fight in the name of love requires entirely different means than those others want to impose on us!

We have become strangers, yet our hearts and feelings must not grow cold.

It does not matter to me whether we were born of the same womb or are related by blood. This book carries the experiences of thousands of women.

Women who, like me, were on the verge of being uprooted and had to find their place in life through tears! Home — let me tell you this — is only known to those in exile; all others are simply at home! Today, my home is Germany, but in my heart, I will forever be a Persian who painfully misses her homeland.

"Well, you must be glad to be here now..." is the most heartless question one can ask me. That is why I want you to know everything about me and see yourself in my story!

Faithfully yours

Afsaneh

For a long time, Afsaneh knew that she wanted to bring these lines to the world. But who would understand them?

Not only women — all people should feel the strength gifted to us, to love one another and offer protection. "Love is the bridge between you and everything else." This was the teaching of Persian poets, above all Jalal ad-Din Muhammad Rumi, whom many simply call Rumi. He was not lacking in wisdom. "Maybe in internet access," her granddaughter once joked. "Today, he'd be a popular influencer!" Rumi's words gave Afsaneh strength in a world where the powerful could turn off the internet whenever it suited them. But not in the whole world, and certainly not in Germany, where she had now lived for nearly 50 years.

Afsaneh looked at these first pages with dissatisfaction. She wanted to read lines about her pure feelings, but how? Didn't it require a new kind of dialogue, one in which people didn't lose their identity? How do we share our feelings?

Much had already been demanded universally and technically in terms of rights, which people ultimately refused to grant each other. What contribution could she, as a grandmother, make to the so-needed dialogue among people today?

She wanted to use her voice because she could. In a very concrete way, she wanted her story to remind people of what is often the most powerful driver of change: feelings! Emotions that make us one with the moment. Primeval human feelings shared with others — love, joy, and also anger — that open our eyes and allow us to look beyond the surface of things.

Her granddaughter herself had no chance to travel freely with her through the country where she had spent a happy childhood. Instead, they followed the news on their smartphones about the anniversary of the death of the young, Kurdish Jina 'Mahsa' Amini, who had become a symbol of the Women-Life-Freedom movement worldwide. Another daughter, sister, and friend whose life, like a single drop, fell into the ocean of men and women who had died, refusing to be controlled.

Tears, often mocked as mere drops, sometimes spark movements that displease the powerful and serve as an example to others. Afsaneh had no idea that in October 2023, the EU would award the Sakharov Prize for Freedom of Thought to *Women-Life-Freedom*, nor that the imprisoned human rights activist Narges Mohammadi would receive the Nobel Peace Prize from the Swedish Academy, becoming the second Iranian woman after Shirin Ebadi to do so. Yet she sensed that all this international attention would embolden the haters in their system of disdain and destruction of life.

No other country on earth had been subject to such human-driven change from the beginning as her homeland, Persia, for 6,000 years now. A land rich in traditions and struggles, "neither East nor West," which could be a school for the world in hospitality, comfort, sustainability, and religious tolerance.

She was weary of answering the same questions about her homeland over and over again. Questions she herself could not answer, and which burned within her more fiercely than any questioner could ever grasp.

When she grew up in Iran in the 1960s, her peaceful country radiated its Persian culture across the world. "Her country" had been a founding member of the UN. The Cyrus Cylinder was considered the first declaration of universal human rights. With this heritage, one could hold one's own anywhere in the world, equipped with the inner resources for a good life. But then her homeland changed, and other images and stories became associated with the word Iran. Far from home, she found it increasingly difficult to convey what made her country so magnificent.

"Her country" was now Germany, but in her heart, she remained a Persian.

Even today, she could still feel her dismay, remembering herself sitting beside unpacked suitcases in Hamburg. Her first husband no longer deemed it "safe" to live in Iran. She had married this German out of love, a man who had felt for the first time in Iran that he could breathe freely. And yet her homeland was no longer to be her home?

She felt a homesickness she had never known, as she stared out from her furnished apartment at the leaves the wind tore from the summer-weary trees. Trees so tall one could have climbed to the heavens. The only thing she cared about was the sun of Iran, and now this light was suddenly so far away.

In her entire childhood, she had never known fear. Growing up in a large family surrounded by a handful of wild boys, there was no challenge she hadn't faced. While she couldn't live in the past, what would her new life in Germany offer? What about the people? Where were the familiar ones, those with whom she could laugh and cry? Just people who would take her in their arms and invite her into their homes?

She knew no one yet, not even her in-laws in Germany. Everything was foreign.

Worse yet, everything was cold. The colors of her youth would fade in this cold country, and for the first time in her life, she felt doubt. Always ready to take things as they came without overthinking, she had no idea how much she would suffer. The cool politeness with which many people in Germany encountered each other startled her. It would take her much energy to preserve her own nature.

"The bird of patience flies slower, but it reaches further."
Der Vogel der Geduld fliegt langsamer,
aber dafür weiter.   • Rumi

Her gaze fell again on her smartphone and the shocking news from Iran. Another girl dead. Killed because men thought she had worn her headscarf improperly. Men who had once felt so plagued by the West that they insulted those who thought differently — even their own mothers, sisters, and daughters — as "prostitutes" and declared every protest by women illegal. The violence they unleashed eroded hope for a better coexistence.

Whenever she wished, Afsaneh could feel the wind in her hair, and yet she was not free. The language of her heart was not the language the people around her understood. First English, and after difficult years, German were the words she could share with those around her. She would have withered inside if not for the language of Persian poets, which continued to refresh her spirit. "The word that comes from the soul will certainly reach the heart!"

Though she could still travel freely with her two passports, like a bird, the changes she observed over the decades in her homeland weighed on her more and more. So much had the people lost, and once-flourishing landscapes had withered. She longed for her granddaughter to one day breathe in the richly scented air of Iran, as her daughter once had, and look into the proud eyes of her relatives. "The future is unwritten!"

The path to God, Rumi had warned 800 years ago, can only be walked through love. Today, she felt more than ever the deepest desire of her people: to live in peace and friendship with the entire world!

Who could she find to put her words on paper? Someone who understood her language. The language of her feelings and thoughts beyond the words in a language that was not the language of her heart.

Her granddaughter could do it, but she was still too young. She had to go in search, for people in Germany needed to understand what it means to be Persian.

"Beyond right and wrong, there is a field. We'll meet there."

Jenseits von richtig und falsch
da treffen wir uns   • Rumi

Beyond right and wrong, there is a field.
We'll meet there.

Dschalāl ad-Dīn Rūmī, zitiert aus:
Gewaltfreie Kommunikation,
Paderborn 2003

As a
Persian writing Scholar,
Rumi (1207-1273 CE),
also known as Maulana
or Mevlana,
lived
in several locations
within a multicultural
environment,
influenced by the
expansion of the
Mongol Empire.

He rejected any boundaries or division among people. Thoroughly trained in the traditional sciences, Rumi studied and taught in Konya — a city in present-day Anatolia — where he formed a deep friendship with Shamsuddin. He followed the urge to write poetry and composed over 60,000 verses. Among his major works are the *Masnavi*, *Diwan*, and *Fihi Ma Fihi*, some of which were dictated to his students and have since inspired numerous interpreters.

In his second marriage to a Christian, his focus of inquiry became the spiritual realm of faith: love as the primary force of the universe.

"I sought him on the cross of the Christians,
but he was not there. I went to the temples
of the Hindus and the ancient pagodas,
but nowhere could I find a trace of him.
I searched for him in the mountains and valleys,
yet neither in the heights nor in the depths
was I able to find him. I went to the Kaaba in
Mecca, but he was not there either.

I questioned the scholars
and philosophers, but
he was beyond their
understanding.

I looked into my heart, and
there he dwelled,
as I saw him there.
He is to be found
nowhere else."

My
Notes

I felt as though I knew nothing about Iran.
How could that be?

I looked helplessly at the neat lines of this brave woman and the small strip of paper in my hand, which I had initially thought was a fortune cookie message. I had studied Avicenna and other Neoplatonic writers, but why did I know nothing about this Rumi?

It wasn't hard to google the background of this Persian scholar from the 13th century. In fact, a rivalry had flared up over him, who was known by many names, between Afghanistan, Iran, and Turkey, each of them asserting their right to preserve his heritage at UNESCO. Woman, Iran, Rumi... I still puzzled over whether and how I, as a German, could possibly help.

With its colorful history, Iran was by no means comparable to its neighbor Afghanistan; that much was somehow clear to me, even though the images of the last forty years conveyed a dangerous half-knowledge.

After some initial internet research, I went to a very large bookstore in an international German city and asked for a travel guide on 'Iran'. Astonished looks were all I received. After all, it wasn't desirable to travel to Iran as a tourist. Not desirable?! Shouldn't I, couldn't I, or wouldn't I even want to… in the 21st century?

It was all the more fascinating how Rumi in the 13th century — free from any notion of national identity — lived in a multicultural metropolis like Konya and there, across religious boundaries, explored the human capacity for faith and love. I wondered what it was like for Afsaneh, growing up in the Iran of her childhood. What does she really mean when, after introducing herself over the phone, she says with a proud voice: "I am *Persian*!"

Walking through life with blind spots goes strongly against my German, Protestant upbringing. Since World War II, a lack of knowledge has been considered a form of complicity. Wanting to understand cultures, beliefs, and human coexistence has been ingrained in me since my school days.

As a sturdy, blonde girl, I started asking myself early on which chords the Nazis might have struck in me if I had been born in 1927 instead of 1972?

Not exactly by choice, as I remembered while writing down these notes: In our high school, we had a traveling exhibition on the extermination in the concentration camps between 1936 and 1945. Faced with countless photos of mutilated and buried bodies of the dead, I couldn't hold back my tears. A chubby, dark-haired classmate responded to me:

"Why are you even crying? With those blue eyes of yours, you wouldn't have had anything to fear under the Nazis!"

With his words, which held as much insight as fear, he mocked my compassion. Words that struck me deeply. Neither my country of birth, nor my era, nor my appearance were a choice of my own.

Would I have held any power as a 12-year-old in that dreadful time?

How does one confront villains who present their own well-being as the welfare of the people, their own profit as national progress? Who invoke nation, though the lives and freedom of their compatriots mean nothing to them? How does one handle the responsibility of not becoming the target of persecution or discrimination oneself?

How to resist the temptation — to elevate oneself above others when circumstances allow — is a question that troubles people worldwide. The political situation in Iran has never been solely the concern of those whom the Greeks, after their conquest, called Persians.

In Europe's narratives, an "enlightened West" is often contrasted with a "mysterious Orient." How seriously did the world take a culture shaped and constrained over many centuries by Muslim rulership, yet one that sought to implement a peaceful, constitutional government, while Europe was busy with two world wars? What are we leaving to our children if we content ourselves with what our civilizations have managed to produce so far? Travel restrictions, sanctions, and deep cultural mistrust?

With the ignorance about Iran and its Persian culture comes the risk of losing the understanding that cultural identity is a gift, not a stigma.

If our strength continues to wane, it will fall to our children and grandchildren to defend this world we so enjoy living in. Misunderstanding and lack of knowledge will not help them.

Afsaneh's aim to give future generations insight into her own history could be my aim as well. Why not walk this path together? What kind of story could this become? What assumptions are already embedded in our experiences?

Nation-states, much like city societies, are a joy for historians as human creations.

Jurists are even more delighted: After all, borders make it much easier to establish binding legal systems — whoever might enforce them — and to ensure the enforcement of these rights and duties — whoever might oversee it.

"City air makes you free" became, in historical accounts, a symbol of progress for many — a vision of how great things supposedly were in the Middle Ages: escaping the arbitrary rule of the feudal lord and settling in the city with one's skills and talents.

Forgotten, however, are the centrifugal forces of a confined city society that have always driven individuals to move on and even entire peoples to migrate. In the West, we use the term "motivation" after the Latin 'movere', which means 'to initiate movement'. It doesn't necessarily imply voluntariness.

With social density comes social control. The multitude of regulations — from dress codes, building codes, and marriage licenses to professional permits, taxes, and levies — made city life anything but a piece of cake, even in earlier centuries. However, life in the city often brought great hardship and suffering as well.

And while "civilization" (another one of those Latin terms) by definition actually refers to the development of coexistence, aiming to create a peaceful and aggression-free way of life, it often fell short of this ideal.

One might assume that, due to its climate, the Middle East is fundamentally a world of cities. For outside of cities or civilization, human survival is arduous, if not nearly impossible — a truth conveyed through countless stories in the Bible.

And it's not only the Bible; our entire historical record is filled with tales of the rise and fall of human-made orders. Our nature inclines us to tell history through little histories. Stories that moves us.

While men in the Western world have always written about wars and political customs, the past 200 years have seen a growing number of different stories — stories about how people, both men and women, grow beyond their origins. Often, a change of place is just the first step. Love and marriage become the driving forces for emancipation and the creation of a life perspective full of room for innovation. With 70,000 new German books published every year, it hardly seems worthwhile to write yet another such story. Another genre novel in the hum of letters and words makes no difference. No, that's not the story we're writing!

As a young girl, Afsaneh was born into a culture she found healing and beautiful. But the changes in her homeland alienated her, along with more than five million people worldwide who no longer live in Iran (or no longer wish to). What remains is her boldly spoken greeting: "Hello, my name is Afsaneh, I am Persian" — and all the uncertainty that comes with it: What does the person across from me know about my homeland, about Persia and the people who live there? What question will I be asked next?

Political decisions, revolutions, and exclusion shape the perception of what, in another time, she regarded as healing and good. According to the Persian, Zoroastrian faith, this quality must be renewed each day through good words, good deeds, and good thoughts. It was not change that caused Afsaneh to suffer, but rather the fixation on an assumed cultural identity.

"Politics is a dirty business," Afsaneh grumbles on the phone during our first call. I wince inwardly, pained by the thought: *Nothing is unpolitical.* The very moment we influence another person's life, we exert power, whether we intend to or not. Power structures are mirrored in every family, reflecting and reinforcing societal hierarchies, with the most vulnerable often bearing the weight of this influence. Children absorb these dynamics early, learning what they are to regard as right and good.

With power comes responsibility. Rumi was fascinated by the power of love. National interests would have amused him. He was drawn to the invisible bonds that move us and bring us into harmony — what people in the West often like to call mystical. In Western culture, it's important to draw clear lines between concepts, often without sensing the power that comes with such precision. Through the use of words, a well-intentioned term can quickly become a stigma.

"You, woman!" was a teasing term of endearment among us girls in my youth, as we dealt with our first menstrual discomforts. It was our way of parodying gender labels that we no longer felt applied to us.

Feminism was yesterday? We thought the world was ours! How we use language is always in motion. The language of our own cultural sphere eventually becomes boring once we've learned to speak correctly. Teenagers still enjoy decoding terms and adding new codes to existing language, while older people often resort to other languages, eras, and cultures to avoid losing the joy of conversation and exchange.

Wanting to look beyond the surface is not only allowed but a sacred duty for us humans. All prophets call for inward reflection, and in the Bible, Paul sighed in his letter to the Galatians 5:21, that the rest was just *feasting and drinking*. The everyday becomes banal at some point. Yet within each ordinary act lies a spark of what we call culture — a part of ourselves that shapes our identity. When we confront our own mortality, we begin to wonder: What will remain?

It wasn't hard for me to respond to Afsaneh. In cultural exchange, one is supposed to speak with each other, not about each other. That's exactly what she has done for almost fifty years in Germany — as well as in her homeland of Iran. And that's what makes it so rewarding to listen to her and to engage in dialogue together.

Im Vergleich Deutschland

Iran?!

Crossing trade routes between the ends of the known world brought wealth to the region until the 14th century.

After the Romans, who brought Latin into the Celtic and Germanic cultures of what is now England and Germany, people began to distinguish their movement: toward the Land of Dawn or the

Land of Morrow.

Before you speak,
let your words
pass through
three gates.
Are they true?
Are they necessary?
Are they kind?
• Rumi

Iran currently has a population of over 80 million, similar to Germany, with most people living in cities. However, the average population density is only 50.7 people per km².

It wasn't always
this way:
in 1960,
75 % of the population
worked in agriculture,
with a total population
of 20 million.

Known as qanats, early irrigation systems made it possible even before **2000 B.C.** to water the warm highlands, enabling the cultivation of legumes, nuts, cotton, and fruit, as well as wheat, barley, and rice, thus facilitating the nourishment of large populations.

With each empire that came and went, the **multi-ethnic land** experienced shifts in governance, including the unification of tax systems, as well as frequent wars. Yet these transitions also fostered an unyielding spirit of innovation. Connected to thriving markets, the people became highly skilled in the production of goods like textiles, carpets, and ceramics. However, in a largely oral culture, formal education remained a privilege afforded to only a few.

Our Dialogue

Thank you, my dear Afsaneh, for inviting me to this exchange!

Afsaneh: *Writing a book is more work than I thought. It all feels rather daring, doesn't it?*

Yes, I still have enormous respect for writing. To make people laugh or cry with words…

Afsaneh: *That does sound quite serious. So, why do we do this?*

It's about our experiences and the emotions connected to them. Books can surprise us like people do, but they also offer us a safe space for our feelings. As pure and true as only books can tell it all. A place where we are free to define the context.

Afsaneh: *Are you still talking, or are you already writing?*
(we both laugh)
So, reading nourishes the soul?

As does writing! Anyone who speaks is already drawing upon their life. We mirror meaning, reflecting how we see things. But then, each reader brings their own interpretation, literally transforming the text.

From a scientific perspective, there's nothing more important to write down than what readers *read between the lines* and discover in their own thinking.

Afsaneh: *Then it has nothing to do with us at all?*
I don't understand. All this effort ...

Maybe it will make sense to you when you read our book later. With the speed of search engines, we now have access to an incredible amount of information

But in conversation, we have the opportunity to weigh things carefully. We get to know each other, allowing us to deepen our understanding of complex concepts and the thought processes of others.

Afsaneh: *Honestly, you're exhausting. Can someone actually read too much in life?*
I thought we'd just chat a little, and so on. But I see now, this writing business requires a lot of patience.
Come on, let's get started!
You must have prepared some questions:
Where shall we begin?

In Iran, even in 1975, 63 percent of the population still couldn't read or write. Did you know that?

Afsaneh: *Dear friend, no, I was just a child! For me, it was completely normal to go to school in Tehran. Like everyone in my neighborhood went to school.*
We had nice, modern schools with free snacks and lunch.
We wore school uniforms, and since it was always so warm, I usually wore a miniskirt.
Did you know that the Iranian parliament passed a law in 1963 to establish the 'Army of Knowledge', which was awarded the UNESCO Education Prize in 1972?

Touché,
I didn't know that! I see, I really have a lot to learn if I want to understand more about you and your homeland. It sounds like life in Iran was...

Afsaneh: *Stop, stop, stop... before you go any further!*
Life in Iran was never just one way or another.
For one thing, it depended on where you lived — in the countryside or in the city, which family you were born into, how old you were, what you believed, and which class you belonged to.
I grew up in the 1960s in the capital of a country that fascinated the world. That's what I can speak about!

Your family is the foundation of all your strength. Your father was an academic. A gift or a burden?

Afsaneh: *Clearly: a gift! Not just my father — everyone in his family had been scholars and advisors to rulers for nearly 300 years. Books and education were entirely natural,*
and heaven forbid if I wasn't diligent enough. Then I'd immediately get tutoring. But it wasn't like it is today in Germany.

Army of Knowledge (Sepah-e Danesch)

In 1965, the UNESCO World Congress in Tehran declared September 8 as International Literacy Day.

From 1967 to 1976, the Mohammad Reza Pahlavi Educational Award was granted.

Young conscripts, both men and women, who had completed high school with a diploma, were trained as assistant teachers to teach in areas with acute teacher shortages.

The 1970 UNESCO Report noted that, worldwide, in addition to state interventions, support from non-governmental organizations is also needed to promote literacy and bring attention to reading and writing.

In 1968 alone, half a million people in Iran became newly literate, yet the extent to which reading becomes part of daily life also determines access to lifelong learning.

By the late 1970s, a network of universities had been established, which continued to expand even after a temporary closure from 1980 to 1983. Today, over 870 universities, innovation funds, and technology parks nationwide support knowledge- and technology-based Small and Medium-sized Enterprises (SMEs).

Faravahar, the supreme chosen spirit,
who flies from purity, symbolizes
the three core principles of Zoroastrianism:
Good Thoughts, Good Words, Good Deeds.

In covered fire temples, flames were kept
as early as the 9th century B.C., intended,
in Zoroastrian tradition, to burn eternally.
To this day, there are communities and temples in Iran
and surrounding regions that uphold this shared faith.

Afsaneh: With so many children, my parents didn't focus much on what each of us was doing, as long as we were all doing well.

For me, everything I'm learning about Iran feels like a series of contradictions. It reminds me of Rumi again: "Beyond right and wrong, there is a field. We'll meet there." Such globally renowned scientists, writers, and teachers, and yet it wasn't until 1851 that the first modern university, Dar al-Fonun, was established in Tehran.

Afsaneh: The first modern university! The ,List of Persian Inventors and Discoverers' is long — you can look it all up on Wikipedia. But the transmission of knowledge wasn't just accessible to everyone. Just as Rumi first studied with his father and then with Attar, it was long a tradition for students to seek out their teachers. They would live with them, study with them, and search for wisdom. But that's talking about ancient Persia!

Since 1934, Persia has been officially called Iran. The intention was to leave behind the *foreign designation* the Greeks once gave the region and its people, in a very modern move.

Afsaneh: That was the idea. Just like how the Indians pushed for their major city to be called Mumbai instead of Bombay! Well, with Iran, that hasn't worked quite as well. Given what the politicians have done to our country, many Iranians prefer to use the more widespread name 'Persia'.
In any case, the Avestan root 'Airiia' means 'noble', and 'airy-nam' means 'land of the Iranians', which, despite all the foreign domination, reflects a long-standing tradition:

The people's heart, caught between East and West. King Darius referenced this term in his tomb inscription in 486 B.C., directly linking it to the Avesta, the liturgy of the Zoroastrian religion. So forget that crude explanation of 'land of the Aryans,' as many encyclopedias suggest.

The 1930s — a vast field. What can I, as a German, even say about that?

Afsaneh: *Let's get one thing straight: People aren't all the same. You're asking about my school. Why?*

In 2023, so many people know so little about Iran that I almost believe, for many, Iran is just like Afghanistan — only in the past. Both countries were pulled apart by the interests of East and West...

Afsaneh: *... Now, stop right there! That's like equating Germany with Austria or Switzerland. That's absurd! Switzerland only introduced women's suffrage in 1971.*
Persia, for millennia, has attracted people from all over the world with its world-famous cities and provided them with all sorts of goods thanks to its trade routes.

Yes, indeed, quite off-center, in every sense of the word. Let's focus on your life specifically.
You mentioned this yourself when you told me how exhausted you were by the ignorant questions people ask about your homeland.
It made me reflect on why so many Germans have no real concept of life in Iran.
And this, despite us having the internet, international TV channels, and so on today.

Afsaneh: *Well then, why? That's why we're here now, isn't it? And what does that have to do with my school days?*

When people hear about your time as a student in Iran, they understand that you didn't grow up all that differently from kids in Germany.

Afsaneh: *Our fruit at school was much fresher and tastier!*

Of course, it wasn't flown in from some distant country. What was your favorite subject in school?

Afsaneh: *Recess, that was truly the best time.*
I loved math.
We had English as a foreign language, and whenever we met tourists in town, they were always delighted when we could help them!

After primary school, you all attended a co-ed orientation stage from fifth to ninth grade, then came vocational school. And for those who could and wanted to, there was the Abitur. Thirteen years of school is a long time!

Afsaneh: *We had both mixed and separate schools, public and private as well. My last three years were in an all-girls school, which I didn't mind. I had plenty of boys at home: three younger brothers and two nephews. I enjoyed spending time with my girlfriends.*
One afternoon, we didn't feel like going to class, so we went to town instead. There was a new café with delicious cappuccinos. We smoked, flirted a bit with the boys, and had a wonderful afternoon. When I got home, my father was already standing in the street waiting for me!

The letter from school had arrived before I did!
That was how things went in our school.
My father didn't find it funny at all.
He didn't speak kindly to me for at least two days,
but then it was forgotten!

It seems you weren't afraid of anything?

Afsaneh: *Not of my family! We were always kind to each other.*
My father was very disciplined, but I learned a lot from
him. And my mother was my greatest role model!

I think we have that in common: Our parents always resisted sugarcoating things that weren't good.

Afsaneh: *My parents were my teachers for life, and even in their*
old age, they had a keen eye for the world, thanks to their
many travels. Through them, we met so many different
people.
Even after we were grown up, they took the time for each
of us siblings, carefully planning their visits so we all
experienced something special.

What was your favorite snuggle buddy as a child?

Afsaneh: *My mother's or sister's arm.*
Whenever I had a problem, I could always go to them. My
mother never worked outside the home. She was simply
happy to be there for us.

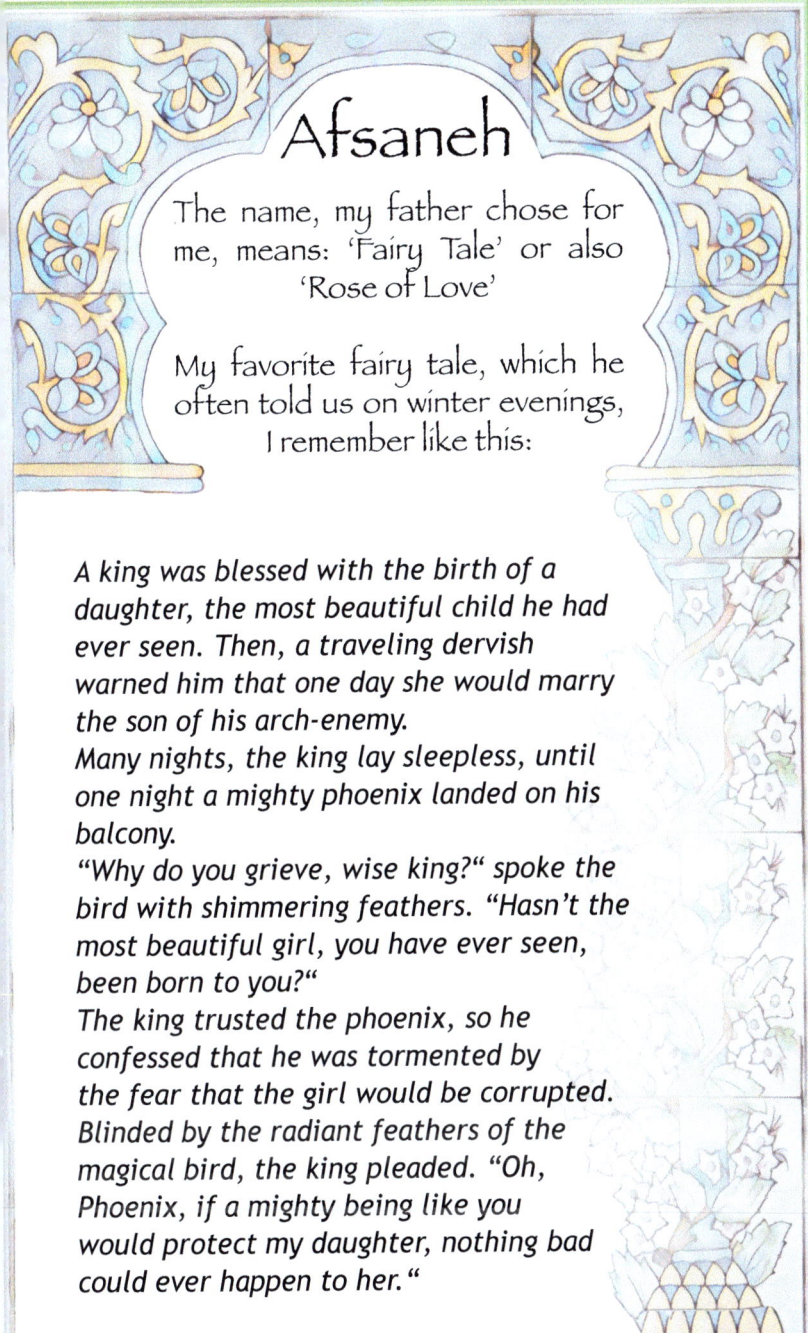

Afsaneh

The name, my father chose for me, means: 'Fairy Tale' or also 'Rose of Love'

My favorite fairy tale, which he often told us on winter evenings, I remember like this:

A king was blessed with the birth of a daughter, the most beautiful child he had ever seen. Then, a traveling dervish warned him that one day she would marry the son of his arch-enemy.
Many nights, the king lay sleepless, until one night a mighty phoenix landed on his balcony.
"Why do you grieve, wise king?" spoke the bird with shimmering feathers. "Hasn't the most beautiful girl, you have ever seen, been born to you?"
The king trusted the phoenix, so he confessed that he was tormented by the fear that the girl would be corrupted. Blinded by the radiant feathers of the magical bird, the king pleaded. "Oh, Phoenix, if a mighty being like you would protect my daughter, nothing bad could ever happen to her."

The bird promised the king to always take good care of the child and took her with him.

So the girl grew up in a mighty tower
where the phoenix had its nest. Every day,
he took good care of the girl, and her grateful
nature sweetened life for them both.

One day, the girl's hair had grown so long that,
as the phoenix circled above, she could use it to
climb down from the tower.
At the foot of the tower was a lake, where she
saw her reflection for the first time. As her eyes
absorbed every detail of herself, another face
appeared on the surface of the water.
A prince,
who had been searching for the legendary daughter
of the king, stood behind her, and they fell in love
as soon as they turned to face each other.
Despite all obstacles, the princess married the son
of the king's arch-enemy, and they were happy
until the end of their days. The phoenix, however,
was glad that the girl had never been corrupted.

What was your mother's daily routine like?

Afsaneh: *By 9:00 a.m., she always had the meals for the day prepared. She loved cooking, and since she had help around the house, she could devote herself to what mattered most to her. The door to her home was always open, and people visited each other freely. When you met someone, you'd already plan to spend the weekend together.*
Eating and drinking, enjoying beautiful music, simply having a good time — this was the foundation to make everyone feel comfortable. Creating space for good conversations, thoughts, and plans. I always wanted to live like that!

My mother was a ‚housewife' in the 1980s, but I never wanted that!

Afsaneh: *Back then, I didn't know what life in Germany would be like! Always cleaning, and no one has time.*

Oh, so people don't have to clean in Iran?

Afsaneh: *Of course they have, but housework is done together. Like almost everything.*

That reminds me of how our term "family" comes from the Latin 'familia', which means household community. It didn't originally mean father, mother, and child as it's practiced today — or, even more difficult, a single parent raising children alone.

Afsaneh: *In Iran, it was normal for households to be communities. You lived, ate, and laughed together. You were never as alone as people are here.*

Headscarf or no headscarf?

Afsaneh: *My goodness, what a question! Have you ever been in a really hot region?*

Never without a head covering! I prefer a scarf — it's the most practical!

Afsaneh: *Where were you born again?*
> *(We laugh together, despite the bitterness.)*

In the middle of Germany. Under strong sun, I quickly turn into a blonde tomato. Even in Greece, I never went through the midday hours without a headscarf.

Afsaneh: *When the old Shah tried to enforce a headscarf ban, my grandmother argued with every policeman she met. She loved her headscarf.*

Isn't it remarkable how men think they can tell women what to wear.

Afsaneh: *Dress codes don't only affect women, you know, … !*

I find it horrifying how quickly youth embraces dress codes. It doesn't matter where you look; it's all about having the right style or brand — otherwise, you're treated like a second-class citizen.
And now, we've moved seamlessly from headscarves to tyranny.

Afsaneh: *Tyranny of fashion is not the same as dictatorship! You know we're not just talking about a piece of fabric here!*

Wearing a head covering often gains acceptance faster than showing one's own hair.

Afsaneh: *Bad Hair Day! But I don't want to joke about this.*

Have you ever considered how, before showers became common worldwide, it wasn't always easy to achieve the hairstyle you wanted, depending on your hair type? Across all cultures, people have always chosen head coverings voluntarily, depending on the occasion.

Afsaneh: *Somehow, people seem to have forgotten that emancipation wasn't a gift from men to women. All over the world, including in ancient Persia, women fought for the right to make decisions about their own bodies and everything that comes with them.*

I know who you're thinking of. The influence of the Bahai religion on the European women's movement in the 19th century is a fascinating research topic. Let those interested look it up online!
With the right questions, our perceptions change too. Some people forget that gender discrimination doesn't only affect women.
Let's get back to your childhood. What was that like for you in Iran?

Afsaneh: *We never excluded anyone. On the contrary, our home was always open.*
When Christians moved in across from us, my mother invited them to our garden. She said, "See, we're joyful and love to celebrate even without alcohol!" The girl became my best friend, and we spent several school years together.

Were all families in Tehran like that?

Afsaneh: *Every family was different. Sometimes women from the neighborhood who didn't go out much invited us over to celebrate.*

That happened too? So, it wasn't just miniskirts and French cafés?

Afsaneh: *I've told you before, there wasn't just 'one life in Iran'! But regardless of how people lived, they had opportunities for a good life.*
Hospitality and good manners aren't just a matter of money. Even in the smallest homes, where there is love, it's possible to make the best of things. As Rumi said: "The best moment is now!"

That sounds wonderful if people can live like that.

Afsaneh: *Warmth and love!*
It's not just about enjoying each other's company but also the food — beautiful summer fruits, healthy things, not just coffee or something alcoholic. For Persian women, it's a joy when guests come over.

Tell me
about the other women in your neighborhood.

Afsaneh: *Even during the Shah's time, there were families who suppressed their daughters.*
Different traditions lived side by side. On the streets of Tehran, you could see everything: miniskirts, trousers, headscarves, and fanatic clothing. It was a colorful mix.

No one said anything to anyone else about it.

And how was it for you when you visited these other families?

Afsaneh: *As long as we were children, we just played together in the garden while the mothers and aunts sat around a big, beautifully set table.*

Everyone brought food. It was always delicious. First, a preacher, whether a man or a woman, would come and recite verses from the Quran. No one really understood them because they were in Arabic.

Then, everyone would cry a little over the sadness of what was read, give donations, and the preacher would leave. But the women stayed, chatting about their families and marriages.

Really, they cried together?

Afsaneh: *The preachers often chose sad stories, like the death of the Prophet or similar passages. Everyone would get very emotional. The women cried, and in a way, it was therapeutic, because by the end of the evening, it was simply a shared event.*

Once, a woman cried so much that my mother whispered to me that she wasn't crying for the Prophet but because of her own problems.

These gatherings were open to all women, and that's why the community was so important. Tears were often followed by laughter and shared joy.

As I got older, I started to feel uncomfortable at these gatherings.

I was just grateful to grow up in the family I did.

Strong Women
made in Iran

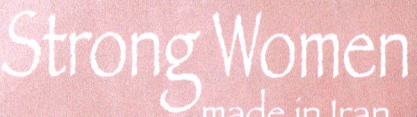

Shirin Ebadi, *June 21, 1947, in Hamadan studied law, 1975-79 Chair of the Tehran City Court as the first female judge in Iran to this day, she remains a lecturer and human rights activist.

2003

Nobel Peace Prize

WINNER OF THE NOBEL PEACE PRIZE

2023

Narges Mohammadi, *April 21, 1972, in Zandschan studied physics, loves mountaineering, also an author

In 2011, Ebadi served on the UN competition jury, which selected ten designs from 15,300 proposals for a **new human rights logo** to be voted on online.

"All human beings are born free and equal in dignity and rights."
Universal Declaration of Human Rights, 1948, UN, A/RES/217/A-(III)

I think it's amazing that you were able to experience those families firsthand.

Afsaneh: *I grew up in a free family, but I knew that at that time, there were many families where women weren't free. Where women and girls were sometimes even beaten and oppressed.*
Without those families, there never would have been a revolution in Iran. There were so many differences — poor, rich, free, restricted, rural, urban — and all these people carried their unique stories.

So many different lives and stories came together, and yet, at that time, the entire population of Iran was just 20 million people. Today, that number has grown to four times as many. Sometimes, being alone can be refreshing.

Afsaneh: *Then you take a walk. Isn't that normal?*

Well, in Germany, it's *normal* that 41 percent of all households are single households.

Afsaneh: *I didn't know that until I lived in Germany. Honestly, it's completely impractical.*

For any society, it would be good if people could live together with respect and affection.
In Africa, there's a saying: "If you want to raise a child, you need a village."

Afsaneh: *Even in a city, that's possible. You just need to foster community and togetherness. That can only happen with people. Demanding it alone isn't enough!*

Persia becomes Iran

1906 Proclamation of the Constitution
1911 Constitutional Revolution
1917 October Revolution in Russia
1921 Defense against the Persian
 Socialist Soviet Republic
1924 Disempowerment of Khuzestan
 Reza Khan becomes Head of State
1925 Law on 'Identity and
 Personal Status'
1925 General Edu. / Military Service
1926 Coronation of Reza as Shah
1927 Judicial System Reform
 Establishment of the National Bank
1928 Civil Code
1932 Revocation of Oil Concessions
1935 Name change 'Iran' internat.
1936 'Liberation of Women' from
 the Veil (Chador)

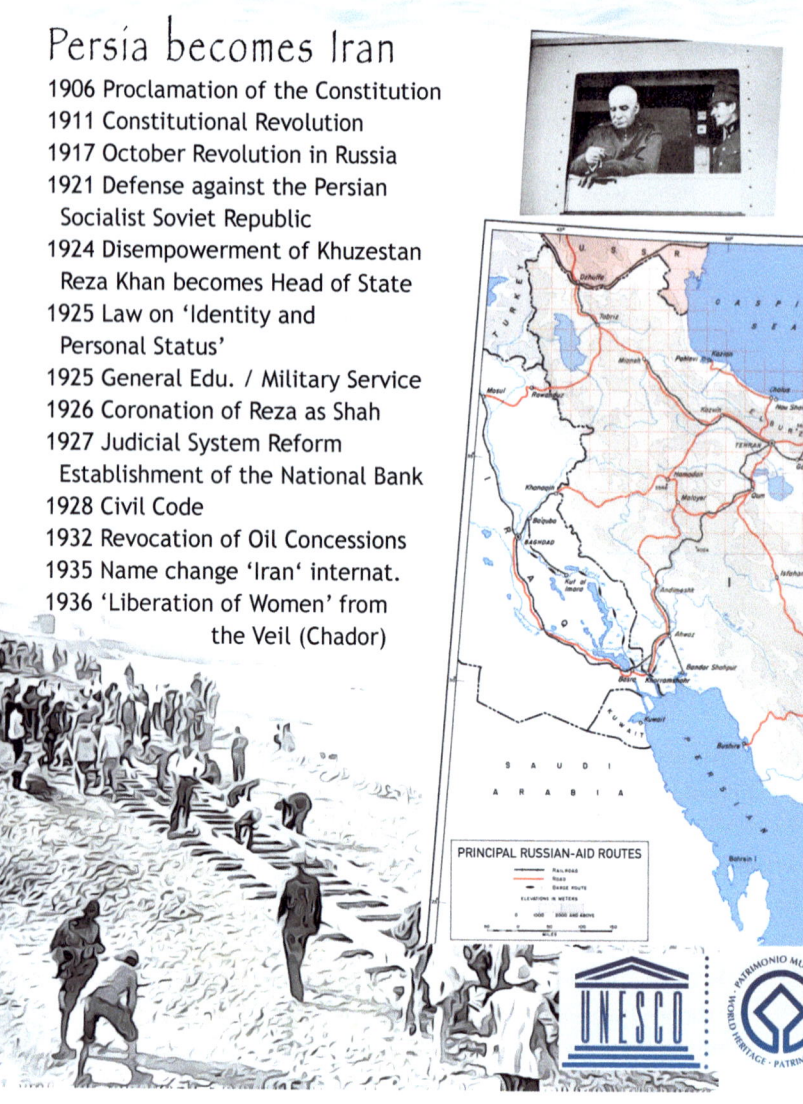

PRINCIPAL RUSSIAN-AID ROUTES

Persia / Iran remained neutral in the World Wars as a founding member of the United Nations. However, starting in 1941, the Allies used the 'Persian Corridor' for four and a half years to supply Russia.

In 2021, the Trans-Iranian Railway was declared a UNESCO World Heritage Site.

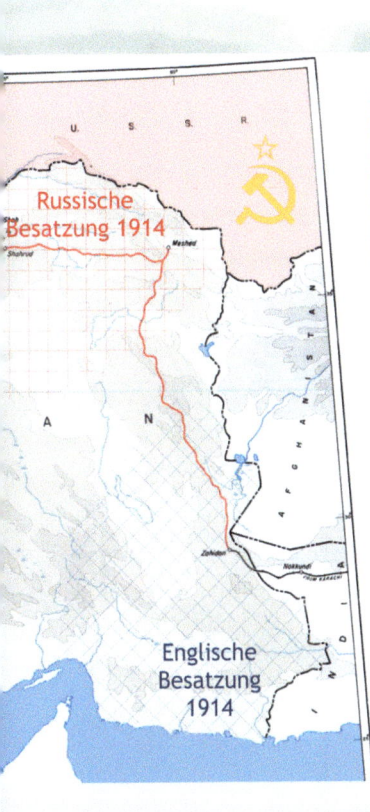

Russische
Besatzung 1914

Englische
Besatzung
1914

Cold War ?!

After Hitler was defeated by the Allies, Stalin refused to withdraw his troops from northern Iran by the agreed deadline in 1946.
Since 1941, the USSR had already had political representation through the Tudeh Party.
U.S. President Truman threatened Stalin with the use of nuclear weapons. Only after appealing to the UN and the renewed granting of oil concessions did the complete withdrawal of Russian troops take place.
The Cold War began.

"Revolution is an invention of the modern age," judges Hannah Arendt in her 1963 work. She proposed the thesis that wars would gradually disappear from the political landscape, with revolutions gaining more influence.

At the same time, Arendt warned that "the men who begin a revolution often long for a restoration".

Did you ever have contact with the police?

Afsaneh: *Of course, they maintained law and order.*

Can you give me an example?

Afsaneh: *One afternoon, I went to the hammam with a friend, and she told me she had once seen the shadow of a man in the roof beams. I thought she was imagining things, but sure enough, there was a student hidden among the rafters.*
We alerted the bath attendant, who immediately called the police. They came and took the guy away.
Why do you ask?

"The police were feared during the Shah's time", is said.

Afsaneh: *My dear, the world has grown a bit wiser since then.*
It's clear now that there are truly people who seek to destroy others. I don't want to make my memories of that time political. Look at the media. You'll find everything there.

'To destroy others' is an important point. Weren't you afraid of Germany?

Afsaneh: *Not at all. The foreigners who came to Iran respected our laws.*
I had no reason to fear any outsider—on the contrary. We were connected to the rest of the world, not only through television. Tehran attracted many foreigners who came to immerse themselves in Persian culture, enjoy its wealth, and seize the opportunities it offered.
Think of the appeal Dubai has today.

People loved the sense of progress, and I even fell in love with a German who was working with an international company in Iran.

So, was it adventure that brought you to Germany?

Afsaneh: *Adventure? Love! But yes, love is also an adventure, with an uncertain outcome.*

What did you expect from Germany?

Afsaneh: *Nothing, really, other than an interesting travel destination. I could never have imagined that one day we wouldn't be living in my homeland anymore.*

Did life in Iran offer you every opportunity?

Afsaneh: *Of course.*

But didn't some of your siblings marry foreigners too?

Afsaneh: *Yes, some of them did. But my husband loved Persia.
I never expected that I would spend the rest of my life in Germany!*

Wasn't he quite homesick?

Afsaneh: *He never talked about that. He had his own color TV, and with so many channels, he could watch programs in German or English, things he was familiar with from back home. Such a rich selection was rare — probably only Japan had something similar.
So, when he wanted to be alone, he had his own retreat.*

But he also enjoyed talking, dancing, and traveling the country.

It must have given you a lot of joy,
to show him everything!

Afsaneh: *We loved just taking a car and hitting the road, traveling light. Once, we even drove all the way from Hamburg through so many countries back to my parents. But then, completely unexpectedly:*
Project canceled! No clinic, no work, no shared future in Tehran.

What did you know about your siblings and friends who had gone abroad?

Afsaneh: *One thing I definitely didn't know was that a minute of a phone call in Germany cost 70 pfennigs — oh yes!*
We were far from today's information age. There was no internet, no smartphones!
I liked what I saw, but I had no idea what kind of life awaited me.

At the time, *Cold War* narratives dominated our media. Over here, we had just two TV channels, ARD and ZDF, and the 'third channels' that aired regional news for a short window in the evening.

Afsaneh: *I wasn't much into TV, that little box. Eventually, every second household had one.*
There were lots of educational programs, and foreign channels aired with subtitles.

As kids, we were mostly outdoors. At home, we had a film room, and when the family got together, we often came up with a program. We even made admission tickets. Watching movies together was a real highlight. My father loved cowboy films.

I don't want to talk so much about my life. There wasn't really much to it. I never had to climb mountains or face threats to my life.
When I came to Germany, people would warmly approach me, smiling, delighted that I took an interest in their country.

Well, national pride isn't exactly something we're comfortable with here. Except maybe during the World Cup and we happen to win, like we did in 2014. In Iran, however, people seem to be raised with a strong sense of pride in their country...

Afsaneh: *Do you think so?*

Did I say something wrong?

Afsaneh: *I don't think my ancestors needed to be taught to be proud of their heritage.*
You simply were who you are. And if you could live a good life, you were just grateful for it.
No one chooses the family they are born into. The whole concept of nation-states is a relatively modern phenomenon.
Anyone can live anywhere, and we Iranians are proof of how adaptable people can be.

Mega City

Isfahan until 17th c.

Once upon a time,

there was a ruler

who wanted the

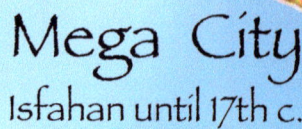

biggest and most beautiful city...

During the time of Shah Abbas I, a strong administration organized the lives of 600,000 people in the former river oasis on the southern route of the Silk Road. Situated 1,500 meters above sea level, a fertile valley sustained the metropolis. More and more labor was needed to maintain a standard of living for people from all parts of the known world, ensuring that no one wanted to leave.

Such a successful city attracted both envy and conquerors.

The loss of talents

Brain Drain

Whether Beijing, Delhi, Hampi, Cairo, Baghdad, Constantinople, or indeed Isfahan, more than 500 years ago, major cities on an unprecedented scale were already attracting people to relocate their lives.

Political conditions and shifts in power often "motivate" people to migrate.

The poet Rumi is just one prominent example from the history of Persia. He spent his life composing poetry in the language of his homeland while living in Konya.

In the 19th century, Prime Minister Amir Kabir sent bright minds to Europe to recruit talent for the "House of Knowledge" he had founded. Foreigners came.
According to legend, his mother-in-law first had him deposed and then murdered. The son of a cook, Amir Kabir systematically dismantled the privileges of the powerful through education.
His strategy
- **intercultural education later enabled the Constitutional Revolution.**

With the Islamic Revolution in 1979, the term "Iranian Diaspora" began to be used, approximately:

240.000 in Germany
85.000 in United Kingdom
35.000 in Netherlands
20.000 in France
20.000 in Austria
20.000 in Denmark
90.000 in Sweden

1.000.000 in USA
280.000 in Canada
out of more than 3.000.000 emigrants.

I probably started this the wrong way, but it's also important to me that our readers get a sense of what you left behind.

Afsaneh: *I didn't feel that way at first.*
I was curious about the world and could travel wherever I wanted, like a bird.
I was young and thought I'd live abroad for a few years. That's nothing unusual, is it?!

But then things turned out differently. For you and not just you ...
Come, let's reminisce about the 1960s for a bit. They were such a beautiful time!

Afsaneh: *Coming from you! You little chick, you weren't even born yet.*

No, seriously, when I see black-and-white photos of my aunts and parents from back then, they all look like movie stars.

(we both laugh again)

Afsaneh: *Well, part of that was certainly*
because people didn't take pictures at all hours with their smartphones back then.
And also, everyone is a child of their time.
The photos of my parents from the 60s looked fantastic too.

You told me your mother had a very special lipstick from Christian Dior and the *Miss Dior* fragrance on her dressing table.
Did that spark your admiration for him?

Afsaneh: *My mother was a woman who knew how to dress beautifully and take care of herself.*
I loved running my hands through her wardrobe, feeling the wonderful fabrics, and soaking in the scents.
When she got ready for a party, I'd sit on her bed and watch her.
To me, she was even more beautiful than Farah Diba!

Ah, so it was the woman, not Dior ...

Afsaneh: *What do you have against Dior? I revere that man. In Paris during that era, he realized after those terrible world wars that women needed hope again.*
That perhaps they themselves were the hope, allowing people to feel young and hopeful once more. It's no coincidence that he left behind political science and diplomacy.

The young Shah equipped his wives with everything money could buy.

Afsaneh: *Farah, who gave him four children, he even made Shahbanu in 1967. But the son of the first Pahlavi Shah wasn't that young anymore.*
He probably already knew about his cancer and was worried about what would happen to his family without him.

In Germany, it was more the childless Soraya who was famous. But even compared to European monarchs, Farah's dedication to her official duties and the way she infused them with purpose is truly remarkable. It's no coincidence that she was chosen to open the international UN Women's Conference in Tehran in 1965!

Influencer

use their presence and
reputation on social networks
to promote lifestyles.

Farah Diba, *1938, who later became the empress
and third wife of the last Shah of Persia, gave him
three children and much happiness in life.
As a youth champion in high jump and
a scout, she was seen as a modern
Iranian woman who embodied
the virtues of modernity,
from social engagement
to voting
rights.

1963
Women's
suffrage

1967
New family law with
extensive rights for women

Fawzia
of Egypt
1921-2013

Cui bono?

from Latin:
Who benefits?

The elites of the Middle East had long studied at European universities, where they met and became acquainted.

The lives of the 'rich and beautiful' fueled the desires of war-torn countries in Europe.

Soraya
1932-2001

Like his father, Mohammad Reza Pahlavi released the women he loved from their relationships through divorce, ensuring their lifelong welfare.

Christian Dior enjoyed dressing the most beautiful women in the world until his death, while Coco Chanel teased: "Why does a woman need a dress that doesn't fit in a suitcase?"

The name PAHLAVI, which Reza Khan deliberately chose as his surname in 1925, is intentional:

The new self-image of Iran is intended to draw on the 6,000-year history of Persia. While the deciphering of the cuneiform on the Cyrus Cylinder may yield other interpretations, it has been regarded as a symbol of universal human rights since the founding of the United Nations

What remains is the international strengthening of Iranian and Ancient Iranian studies.

Encyclopædia Iranica

Afsaneh: *I really don't understand why women in Germany sometimes let themselves go so much. I see older women walking around looking like their partner's twin — the same shoes, the same jackets. Even after so many years in Germany, I still find that strange.*

Maybe they see themselves primarily as individuals rather than as women and enjoy the privilege of wearing whatever makes them feel comfortable. Does it matter that much?

Afsaneh: *It does to me. For me, it's a privilege to be a woman. Not just to bear children or something like that, but to have a sense for beauty and loveliness.*
To turn to things that aren't just necessary or practical, but that define us as human beings!

What I don't understand is how Iran could fall apart like that. You had everything: a cool country, sustainable, millennia-old irrigation systems, the skills to cultivate the land, a constitutional government, a constitutional monarchy, oil wealth...

Afsaneh: *Yes, but not everyone had everything! And nothing is as destructive as envy among people. The idea that someone else is better off than me, which keeps so many awake at night.*
The speed with which my homeland Iran developed confused and frightened many people.

It was a development that the Qajar rulers had long sought to prevent. There was always an exchange with Europe and also with the eastern neighbors.

Afsaneh: *Take a look at the "List of rulers of Iran" online. It goes back to 2550 B.C. — at least as far as we know so far.*
One might think
that Iran has tried every form of government over the generations and has repeatedly had to learn that war is the stupidest thing one can do to one's own people.
The Qajars may have been quite preoccupied with themselves, but at least they didn't instigate internal struggles over resources.

I see that somewhat more critically. The failure to defend their own borders allowed the Russians and British to partially occupy the country with troops.

Afsaneh: *That's your perspective looking back.*
Believe me, the world hasn't grown much wiser. Look at Afghanistan, look at Syria. And don't forget how dearly the "peace order of Europe" was paid for — first in blood, then in euros...

Democracy, with free elections and all that comes with it, is historically quite young, I'll admit, but it's a consequence of the codification of universal human rights ...

Afsaneh: *I've told you,*
I don't want to discuss politics with you!

But we both reject violence as a means to enforce interests, don't we?

Afsaneh: *Of course, I oppose any form of violence. What kind of question is that?*

MEANWHILE, THE COLONIAL POWERS DIVIDED THE WORLD:

Avantgarde, friends!

THE WHOLE WORLD ...?! NO! PERSIA HARVESTED THE FRUITS OF THE DAR AL-FONUM*:

Almost peaceful reform, thanks to parliament! Take that, world!

AHMAD, 12 YEARS SHAH-TO-BE

* HOUSE OF KNOWLEDGE, FOUNDED BY AMIR KABIR, 1851

LIKE A FAIRYTALE? 1925: BEGGAR BOY INSTEAD OF PRINCE

Reza Khan* Pahlavi becomes the new Shah!

*THE LONG-TIME DEFENSE MINISTER WAS NOT ALLOWED TO BE PRESIDENT

*FORMER FINANCIAL MINISTER

Without me*

Mohammad Mossadegh (1920)

Stripped of inherited privileges, Mohammad moves from Paris to Switzerland and earns a doctorate in inheritance law.

BACK IN TEHRAN: ... in 1952, Mohammad, now Prime Minister, writes to parliament:

To many dead politicians

Note:
Persia needs political police force
- Innocence? - **Out.**
- Reform opponents? - **Out.**
- Opponents of the Goverment?
  Removed, even **with violence**

The history of the police in Iran goes back a long way

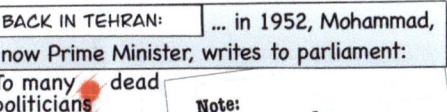

Me too?

No!

Us too ?

... and if you are not dead yet, find the rest on the net!

Afsaneh: *Violence makes me sick. It's simply disrespectful. But your comic reminds me of the images from 1990 when people stormed the Ministry for State Security headquarters of the GDR regime and couldn't believe their eyes at how thoroughly the regime had spied on them and pitted them against each other. Far too many had believed for far too long that they were living in a state of fraternity and solidarity.*

Some people still say this today, telling stories about the 'good old days' ...

Afsaneh: *Because they afford themselves the luxury — and even then allowed themselves — to look the other way!*

For some, it's overwhelming to confront the malice of others. It's as if they hope for a stronger figure to come along and put an end to the villains' schemes.

Afsaneh: *You often read, "The citizens of the GDR managed to peacefully force an end to this politics," as if it had been that simple! Breaking down violent systems requires shared rules and mutual understanding.*
Otherwise, it all ends in even more violence.

When people are in motion, it becomes difficult to control what happens individually.
In Germany, we go to great lengths to keep the memory alive of how things can go terribly wrong in a state.
Whether through memorial sites, museums, or websites like those of the Federal Agency for Civic Education — today, no one can really claim,
"Oh, I didn't know about that!"

Afsaneh: *Just a couple of clicks on the internet, and you're there ... unfortunately, villains also take advantage of this. You must always be vigilant about who you align yourself with!*

"There's only one thing more expensive than education in the long run: lack of education," the saying goes. Whether it's civic education, media literacy, knowledge of other cultures, ways of life, or religions, understanding the basic health needs that enable people to live good and fulfilling lives — all of this must be learned!

Afsaneh: *I'm always glad when my granddaughter comes to talk with me.*
We're often surprised by our differing views, but together we quickly figure out why one of us thinks this way and the other thinks that way.

The history of divided Germany teaches us that you can lie to people for a while, but eventually, there are children and grandchildren who start questioning all these inconsistencies.
Systems that grant privileges to their supporters while fostering inequality and discrimination need enormous energy to suppress the centrifugal forces of such conditions. It's costly in the long run.

Afsaneh: *The GDR simply ran out of money.*
You can't hope for that to happen in every part of the world. So, we have to make the children of this world as smart as possible!
Through my good education, it was easier for me to live in another country.

And yet, you first had to put in all the effort to learn the German language, which is very different from both English and Persian Farsi!

Afsaneh: *Very different! (laughs) Oh yes, I was so young back then, and learning was still just part of everyday life. The language course was quite fun; you immediately got to meet people from other parts of the world. It was exciting to discover how much I didn't yet know about this world.*

Youth makes many things easier. How did your life in Germany begin?

Afsaneh: *My sister arranged a job for me in a boutique, just to get me out among people. And it was exactly the right thing! Much better than cleaning the kitchen — and everything in it — for the hundredth time, even though no guests were coming anyway!*

You preferred "being among people." How was that for you?

Afsaneh: *People saw me as an enrichment, and I could learn the peculiarities of the Germans without being pitied. I was almost a little too modern. Many things here seemed very old-fashioned to me.*
In Tehran, everything was brand new and modern. We had every kitchen appliance, color TVs, slides, films, books, tools, cars. I lacked for nothing. I had everything that seemed useful to me.

You must have seemed very content. I'm glad you could feel so welcome here.

Afsaneh: *Even though you might not be able to imagine this today: People used to cross the street just to talk to me about my background and life.*
No one eyed me with as much skepticism as we tend to feel nowadays.

In Northern Germany?

Afsaneh: *No, (laughs) I know what you mean! Not the cool, distant Northerners.*
Back then, I was living in Wiesbaden, where we had moved so I could be closer to my sister and her family. Everyone was so kind to me.

Nice all the time?

Afsaneh: *I did have to be careful. For many, I was too well-dressed, too neat, too polite.*
I also had to learn how to handle the Germans' more direct way of speaking.

Can you give me an example?

Afsaneh: *When I brought my daughter to kindergarten, the other women would ask, "So, what else do you have planned for today?" I had nothing planned. I had simply dressed neatly. Over time, though, I learned to feel comfortable in sportier clothing.*
As a Persian, you're always very mindful of what you say.

That would benefit many Germans, too. My American host mother once taught me: "If you don't have anything nice to say, it's better to stay silent!"

But honestly, that goes too far for me. It's better to address things at the right time, in a non-hurtful way, than to bottle it up until it explodes!

Afsaneh: *'Nonviolent communication' could have been a great cultural export of Iran.*
Ahimsa, often attributed to the Vedic tradition, has also shaped our Persian culture..

Just as we are capable of love, we are also capable of faith. That's what makes us human.
And even if someone believes in *nothing*, that, too, is an expression of faith.

Afsaneh: *In time, I was happy to return to Hamburg.*
There, over 120 registered religious
and philosophical communities
are accommodated by the Senate's 'religion classes for all'
in schools.
There's no point in always approaching the unfamiliar
through prejudice and stereotypes?

It's easy for you to say!
You've traveled quite a bit!

Afsaneh: *That's true. After a few years,*
I knew more about Germany and the world than many
people who were born here or there! I went everywhere
I could.
My curiosity simply drove me.

Here in Germany, after *reunification*, we could finally grasp what it meant to live through the *Cold War.*

Instead of being able to look into the face of the other, we were always shown the distorted image of the opponent, framed to fit the narrative we told ourselves about the other side.

Not everyone had learned to form their own perspective.

Afsaneh: *After reunification, I was one of the first in my circle to visit all the new federal states.*
Seeing the old, decaying manor houses,
some of which could be bought for a single euro,
made my hands itch!
My dream of running a large house, where guests are constantly coming and going, came alive again!

And then you realized you were living in 1990s Germany, where nobody had time for anything?

Afsaneh: *Something like that! But you don't need a big house to lead a good life. Be at peace with yourself, stand by your talents, and discover what else is within you.*

Travel doesn't just give us space to discover the unfamiliar. Stepping out of our daily routines, we realize what we're truly capable of.

Afsaneh: *My parents taught me that continually questioning your own habits makes you more mindful. In Germany, I discovered a lot that, at first glance, didn't seem very inviting. But as long as something is authentic, you can cultivate even the smallest things into something remarkable.*

When we see images of Tehran in the 1960s, it feels like a glimpse into the future?

Afsaneh: *Treating the past as a vision of the future only leads to confusion. We can only truly meet each other in the 'here and now'.*
Today's images of people in Iran make us think they are from another century. But they're not!

I'm grateful we can have this kind of conversation here. Isn't it remarkable what stories people have to share, especially those who weren't born in Germany like me?

Afsaneh: *It's more a twist of fate where someone is born.*
But the idea that families should support
and hold each other together should matter everywhere in the world.

"If you can't be with the one you love, love the ones you're with," my neighbor in Boston once told me, and there's a lot of wisdom in that. Not every family is as loving, supportive, and enduring as the one you were fortunate to have.

Afsaneh: *"Where there is love, there is no I," Rumi reminds us.*
In a family, you don't ask what the family can do for you but what you can do for the family. That's how you learn what you're truly capable of, and it makes you strong. Until you're ready to start your own family.

Family is what we make of it?
Honestly, I didn't imagine having a family of my own would be so complicated. As a competent adult, I thought, how hard could it be?

Afsaneh: *And who helped you the most?*

The love of my mother and the foresight of those with more experience. "As a mother, you must learn to take small steps!" That was probably the most significant advice I received during my children's early years.

Afsaneh: But: *"Tie two birds together; they will not be able to fly, even though they now have four wings."*

Another Rumi quote? You could go on for hours with those, couldn't you?

Afsaneh: *You should read more Rumi yourself! "Grow wise and change!"*

Go ahead, mock me, but I truly do look up everything I can't immediately place. Thanks to books and the internet!
Besides conversations, sometimes it helps to reflect on things yourself?

Afsaneh: *Oh, so that works too, does it? Says the one with all the questions! Is that enough for today? I'm done.*

Straightforward words! I adore that about you ...

Afsaneh: *But of course. You yourself can't stand polite beating around the bush either, can you?*
Wait until I read this tomorrow! Then I'll tell you, "I never said that!"

Yes, I'm afraid so!

(we both laugh)

Take good care of this day,

for it is life — the very life of life.
In its brief course lie all the truths
and realities of existence,
the joy of growth,
the glory of action,
the splendor of strength.
For yesterday is nothing
but a dream, and tomorrow
only a vision.
But today, well-lived, makes every
yesterday a dream of happiness
and every tomorrow a vision of
hope.
Therefore,
take good care of this day.

~ Rumi

Afsaneh: So, is this how our book should end?

Our thoughts are free! Today, anyone can read any book in any language. People no longer need someone to tell them what to think.

Afsaneh: And what about our feelings? And our responsibility as mothers and grandmothers?

Write, Afsaneh, just keep writing! The world needs all of your stories so that politics everywhere can draft the right laws.

Afsaneh: Oh, you and your politics.
In my life, I've written so much,
but never in German ...

Your experiences bring a unique perspective to things, one that only you can share.
All these stories allow us to form a more complete picture of the world we live in.
And our coexistence needs good laws.
Laws that ensure a good life for people, not just more wealth for the few. Only then can we grow together as a global community.

Afsaneh: I've almost given up that hope.

Not me. And I can't wait to read your book!

Afsaneh: Do you always have to have the last word?

(we both laugh)

Here, yes!

When I imagine the life of a writer or poet,
I always picture someone who spends
their entire life writing,
capturing the struggles in society, the
feelings of humanity, and its pains and problems,
weaving them into a story or poem that will endure.

Yes, writers are people who, with curiosity,
shape the emotions of others into words and
images, reflecting them like a melody that sounds
both beautiful and familiar, making it all visible.

For a passionate writer, their own desires, hopes,
and dreams simply fade into the background as
they immerse themselves in the feelings of others,
distilling them into an artwork that will
be immortalized in literature.

The heart of a writer, like a flame sparked by a
gust of wind, opens up, and from it come the most
beautiful sentences in the world.

Afsaneh 1973

Epilogue

"Our transitional generation has the opportunity to pause and fully utilize its capacity for reflection, in order to prepare itself with all its resources for shaping the future."

Maryanne Wolf,

Proust and the Squid: The Story and Science of the Reading Brain, p. 268

At least the German friend had learned a great deal about Iran through Afsaneh. And through all the research, even more about being a woman in Iran.

Far more than she could bear on some days. But looking away was not in her nature once she was touched by an issue. How can one write about the unspeakable? What do we need to know about each other so that personal identity does not become a stigma?

They had put so much down on paper, yet Afsaneh's uncertainty remained — would this help people in Germany and around the world understand her better?

Having grown up as a free, liberal person, she had painfully experienced how a country changes when it is left to the few who seek to shape it with absolute power. What happens to a people when dogmatists aim to rule. What happens to individuals when they are granted privileges they had never known. What happens to the world when a country is left to its unilateral understanding of the state.

"Politics should not be left to others," urged her friend in conversation, and yes, she was right: Complaining about politics without the willingness to engage and influence will not lead to any improvement in conditions.

Of course, everyone likes to reflect on their own life. But where many people come together, reliable rules are needed. Democracy is an attempt to account for the interests of the many. But democracy can be much more than just the sum of its parts. For this to happen, however, it requires people who think and act responsibly!

It is up to the younger generation to do better. Her story can only serve as a reminder of why Afsaneh became what so many people saw in her: a strong Persian!

Addendum:

Dr. Parnaz Kianiparsa & Dr. Sara Vali: Bā ham A1. Persisch für Anfänger, Ernst Klett Sprachen, Stuttgart 2018.

Maulana Dschelaladdin Rumi: Von Allem und vom Einen, übers. Annemarie Schimmel, Diederichs Verlag, München 2020.

Rashin Kheiriyeh: Rumi. Dichter der Liebe, übers. Thomas Bodmer, NordSüd Verlag, Zürich 2023.

Stephan Orth, Samuel Zuder, Mina Esfandiari: Iran. Tausend und ein Widerspruch, National Geographic, München 2018.

Cornelius Adebahr: Inside Iran. Alte Nation, neue Macht?, Dietz, Bonn 2018.

Geschichte der Welt. Eine Jahreschronik in Daten, Fakten und Bildern, Dorling Kindersley, München 2012.

Barnabas & Anabel Kindersley: Kinder aus aller Welt, übers. Anne Braun, Loewe, Bindlach 1997.

Marshall B. Rosenberg: Gewaltfreie Kommunikation, Junfermann, Paderborn 2003.

Maryanne Wolf: Das lesende Gehirn. Wie der Mensch zum Lesen kam - und was es in unseren Köpfen bewirkt, Spektrum, Heidelberg 2009.

Geo Epoche Kollektion: Der Nahe Osten. Vom 15. Jahrhundert bis heute: Die Geschichte einer umkämpften Region, Heft Nr. 30, Hamburg 2023.

Geo Epoche - Das Magazin für Geschichte: Das alte Persien. Die Geschichte eines Weltreichs - von der Antike bis zur Blüte unter den Muslimen. 550 v. Chr. - 1722 n. Chr., Heft Nr. 99, Hamburg 2019.

Geo Epoche - Das Magazin für Geschichte: Das Osmanische Reich 1300-1922, Heft Nr. 56, Hamburg 2012.

Isnogud. Der Großwesir. Die Goscinny- & Tabary-Jahre 1962-1969, Carlsen Comics, Hamburg 2023.

https://de.wikipedia.org/wiki/Liste_persischer_Erfinder_und_Entdecker
https://de.wikipedia.org/wiki/Persischer_Korridor
https://www.un.org/en/
https://www.nobelpeaceprize.org
https://www.iranicaonline.org

Afsaneh, like the author, are literary figures who emerged from countless conversations with women rich in life experience, coming together to offer all readers and young people insights into the facts, feelings, and thoughts of those who live in Germany today.

Vera Ansén

* 1972, was born in Wiesbaden and grew up in Cologne. She studied theater, film, and television studies, pedagogy, philosophy, and even psychology? She still believes that the head is round so that thoughts can circulate more freely.
With her many talents in words and images, she helps others overcome their speechlessness and never forgets: to entertain well!
Stay curious!